We've been home from our road trip for three days and we keep finding new things that Bad Cat has destroyed.

Papa Dad's house Slippers

DESTROYED

My colored Pencils

DESTROYED

Four houseplants

DESTROYED

The Catsitter's pleasant disposition

NEVER. AGAIN.

DESTROYED

But it's really nice to be home. I never realized how much I missed certain things, like having my own space. Not that it wasn't super fun to share a room with Lydia for a month.

I don't know what you're talking about. I am never not a delight to be around.

Things That Have Changed in My Absence

1. My mom brought home a bunch of new stuff from England.

Do you like them? We're also having some furniture shipped over.

Umm... okay.

2. My mom is super-happy, as if she didn't mind being away from Melody and me for a whole month, and she didn't even care that I dyed my hair.

Tra la la, blue hair, whatever!

3. Melody.

jladybugaboo: She did WHAT?!?

goldstandard3000: She HUGGED me.

jladybugaboo: MELODY HUGGED YOU?

goldstandard3000: With her arms! She wrapped her arms around me and told me that she missed me and that she was proud of me for confronting our dad and she liked my hair!

jladybugaboo: And she has NO hair?

goldstandard3000: NO HAIR.

jladybugaboo: This I have to see.

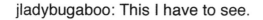

Melody
BEFORE
leaving to build homes in Guatemala
Melody
AFTER
leaving to build homes in Guatemala
Purple hair
Tons of makeup
Piercings
Pale
Cranky
Wacky Clothes
Clunky shoes
NO HAIR!!!
No makeup!
Tan!!!
Tee shirt that used to belong to some boy?!?
Weirdly pleasant
Sandals!
Toe rings?!?

I can't remember the last time that I saw her toes, and now she's walking around barefoot all the time. So. Weird.

What Could Have Happened to Melody This Summer

LOST A BET

If I win, you shave your head.

Sure, whatever.

POSSESSED BY A PLEASANT GHOST

Hallo!

OVERDOSED ON EYESHADOW

If you ever wear eyeshadow again, you'll go blind.

NOOOOOO!

KIDNAPPED BY ALIENS AND REPLACED BY THE NICEBOT 4000

NOOOOO!

These all seem valid. It's hard to choose.

8

The changes are weird, but things are going to change even more because we're about to turn

13!!!

Turning 13 can't be weirder than Melody.

I can't believe you're almost 13. It seems like only yesterday that we were little kids. You are so precious to me.

Who are you and what have you done with my sister?

I value you.

Having both of our birthdays in August is always Laaaaaaammme.

Every year we try to have a party, but our friends are usually away at camp or on vacation.

Roland is in Norway

Lisa is at camp

Jen and her family are in Maine

So we usually have a party with anyone who's around.

It's too bad we're not friends with Gretchen and Jane anymore.

Maybe they'll be friends with us again this year?

Not as long as Jane is dating Chuck.

Why We Can't Be Friends with GRETCHEN and JANE

(It's ridiculously complicated.)

Because Jane is dating Chuck, he isn't allowed to talk to you, because Jane gets jealous.

So you can't be friends with Jane, and because Gretchen is friends with Jane, she can't be friends with you, and since I'm friends with you, both Jane and Gretchen can't be friends with me.

Now, was that so complicated?

Actually, no, just stupid.

Birthday Options

Option #1: BOWLING

Since we're turning 13, we probably can't use bumpers anymore.

Then bowling is out. I don't want to spend my birthday rolling balls down a gutter.

Our parents have offered to take us to New York City for the day, but it takes 2½ hours to get there.

After our cross-country road trip I really don't feel like sitting in a car anymore. No offense.

None taken.

Don't you want to spend EVEN MORE TIME in the car with meeeeee???

A little help here?

Who's my favorite blueberry?

I'm beginning to suspect that our parents offered to take us because they knew we'd say no.

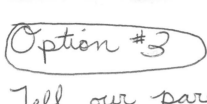

Option #3

Tell our parents that we'd rather have awesome gifts than a party.

Maybe this is the best option. I really, really want my own computer so that I can learn to do computer graphics. Can you imagine how many awesome comic books we could make if I had a computer and a scanner and I could use a font instead of always having to write everything out by hand?

I want to make a comic book about flaming cheese!

I'll be done with that in 5 minutes!

Excellent!

Not that comic books dedicated to cheese aren't awesome, I'm sure they are, but I have a ~~better~~ idea: We ask our parents for

MUSICAL INSTRUMENTS.

Why would we do that?

How would we start a rock band without instruments?

(No Instruments)   (Instruments!)

Sad and lame

AWESOME!

Umm... we don't know how to play music.

BIRTHDAY GIFTS, Part II

Get Music lessons! Think about it — if we get instruments and music lessons, we can totally start a band like the one your cousin Jake had in Ohio.

Jake's so dreamy!

Hush your face, I just respect his talent.

But Jake was in high school. We're just in junior high.

Exactly. If we start learning now, imagine how great we'll be by the time we reach high school. We'll probably be famous by then.

So are we forming a band or what?

I'm still thinking about it, you bug.

you've been thinking about it FOREVER.

It's been less than 24 hours!

That's the entire life span of a mayfly. Think of all the poor mayflies who died in suspense.

Oh for goodness sake.

MY THOUGHTS

(which are valuable and take time to think)
Maybe starting a band wouldn't be the worst idea ever. A lot of people messed with us last year. Maybe if we were in a band, everyone would see that we're cool and leave us alone. Maybe? Plus Jake and his bandmates did seem to be having a great time. Plus Lydia is never going to stop bugging me...

goldstandard3000: Have you talked to your dads about getting you a drum set yet?

jladybugaboo: No.

goldstandard3000: When are you going to do it?

jladybugaboo: I don't know if I even want a drum set. I still kind of want a computer.

goldstandard3000: But you already have a computer. You do not already have a drum set.

jladybugaboo: My dads have a computer, and it doesn't have any graphics programs on it.

goldstandard3000: You can always use the computers at school.

jladybugaboo: I guess so.

goldstandard3000: And being a drummer is great—you get to sit while you play.

jladybugaboo: I do like sitting.

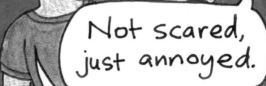

So I hear you're starting a band.

You told her? I haven't even said yes yet.

It's okay. It's good to try things that scare you.

If I hadn't gone out of my comfort zone this summer, I might still be the angry old Melody that you guys were so scared of.

Not scared, just annoyed.

Change is good, my sarcastic little flower.

Maybe Melody is right.

Why do you think Melody went all cranky and gothy when she first got to junior high?

Because she's a great big freak.

No, seriously, why do you think?

I don't know. I guess she was mad at our dad and mad at her friends and just mad and wanted her outside to look like her inside felt. Like a great big freak.

Is that why you dyed your hair blue?

Maybe a little. But then it felt good kind of to do something unexpected.

Let's start a band.

I can't believe you're telling me this in the middle of math class!!!

Could you please stop smiling like a lunatic? I'm trying to take notes.

Nope.

Daddy and Papa Dad were a little surprised when I asked them for a drum set and lessons.

BIRTHDAY WEEK

AUGUST 18th — Lydia's Birthday!
Other things that happened on 8/18

1587 — Virginia Dare became the first English child born in the Americas.

1920 — The 19th Amendment to the United States Constitution was ratified, and women could vote.

But you still have to be 18.

1958 — Brojen Das became the first Bengali to swim across the English Channel in a competition.

AUGUST 24th — My birthday!!!

Other things that happened on 8/24

1891 Thomas Edison patented the motion picture camera.

1912 Alaska became a United States territory.

1932 Amelia Earhart became the first woman to fly across the United States without stopping.

Looking stuff up on the Internet is fun.

I'm pretty sure she had an airplane.

As usual, we went out for brunch with our families on the Sunday between our birthdays.

After brunch we all went back to my house where we found...

OUR PRESENTS!

The drum kit is HUGE. Papa Dad seems excited about it. Daddy bought noise-canceling headphones for both of them.

And next week we're meeting our music teachers!

My Music Teacher

His name is Ryan Mueller and he's going to college for music and he knows how to play about a million instruments.

If he can play the guitar, I don't understand why he isn't my music teacher as well.

MY MUSIC TEACHER
His name is Mr. Merritt, but he wants me to call him "Maestro Merritt" and I'm pretty sure he's eight billion years old. I think my mom found him on an archeological dig.

ladybugaboo: So how did your first guitar lesson go?

goldstandard3000: I don't know if I'm cut out for the guitar.

jladybugaboo: What are you talking about?

goldstandard3000: Maestro Merritt doesn't seem to think that being a rock star is a worthy goal, and it was really hard to get my hand in the right positions, and now the tips of my fingers are all red and sore.

jladybugaboo: Oh no no no. Don't you dare. DON'T YOU DARE. I GOT DRUMS INSTEAD OF AN AWESOME COMPUTER BECAUSE YOU WANTED TO START A BAND AND YOU DON'T GET TO QUIT BECAUSE IT'S HARD.

goldstandard3000: Okay, okay! Calm down, Screamy McAllcaps.

jladybugaboo: Now get offline and PRACTICE.

I can't believe you yelled at me.

BELIEVE IT.

Maybe you need a nap? Practice.

Basic Guitar Chord Hand Positions

 G Chord

ouch.

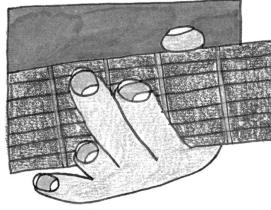

How is my hand supposed to do this?

 C Chord

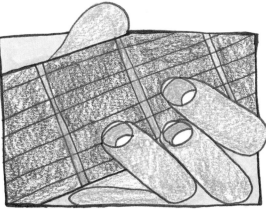

 D Chord

You have it so much easier. you just have to hit stuff with sticks. I'm great at that!

First Day of School Is in

3 Days

goldstandard3000: Are you ready?

jladybugaboo: I guess so. I have all my notebooks and pens and stuff.

goldstandard3000: No, I mean, are you ready for 7th grade?

jladybugaboo: Notebooks, check. Pens, check.

goldstandard3000: Julie!

jladybugaboo: Lydia!

goldstandard3000: JULIE!!!

jladybugaboo: LYDIA!!!! WHY ARE WE YELLING?

goldstandard3000: BECAUSE 7TH GRADE IS DIFFERENT.

What 6th Grade Was Like

You're the youngest in the school, and therefore you are the weakest, like a baby bird that can't fly and is all slimy.

You don't know where anything is, so you believe nearly anything.

The swimming pool is on the third floor.

Really? Neato!

The 8th graders think they know everything and that they're better than you.

Are you dddressing I?

Umm... ho?

What 7th Grade Could Be Like
(If we're properly prepared)

You're no longer the youngest bird in school, so you can fly!

wheeee!

You know where stuff is, so you won't look like a doofus.

By the way, there's no third floor

Good to know.

The 8th graders from last year have gone to high school, where they're the youngest, so we're free not to be intimidated by them!

Who's the slimy baby bird now?

RULES FOR THE FIRST DAY OF SCHOOL

RULE #1: Don't talk to anyone—let them approach us so that we don't seem overly eager.

RIGHT WAY

Hi guys!

Oh, hey.

WRONG WAY

Hi Lisa!

Hi Lisa!

Did you miss us?

We missed you!

We were in California!

And now I own an ugly macramé owl!

RULE #3: No Absurd Schemes to Get Popular, Because They ALWAYS BACKFIRE

I don't know what you're talking about.

I can't believe you're making me sign this.

I, Lydia Goldblatt, do solemnly swear that my desire to start a rock band has nothing to do with being popular. I want to start a rock band because it seems like a fun and awesome thing to do, not a way to impress people. I also promise to practice guitar every day even if it hurts my fingers and my teacher is old and annoying, because I am dedicated to starting this band, which was my idea in the first place.

Lydia Goldblatt

There. I signed it. Happy?

Yep!

The first day back to school is always weird because everyone looks different.

Roland: Taller, shorter haircut.

Gretchen: Blond streak in hair is now pink.

Jen: Has a new vest? Maybe? Something has to be different.

Lydia

You know, I'm so used to your hair being blue that I forget it's kind of freaky to everyone else.

I know! Everyone was staring at me. Even Chuck told me that my hair looked cool.

The best thing about this year is that we have the same lunch period.
And Jen has lunch with us, too.
Vegan brown rice tofu. Want some?
Jane is also in our lunch period. She sits by herself.
Who is she texting?
Probably Chuck.
She's not texting me.
Why would Jane text you?
I thought we were figuring out who she was texting by process of elimination.

Because of our music lessons, our schedule this year is already busy.

Monday	Lydia's lesson with Maestro Merritt, homework
Tuesday	Band rehearsal, homework
Wednesday	Burrito Night, homework
Thursday	Julie's lesson with Ryan, homework
Friday	Just school
Saturday	Band rehearsal
Sunday	Homework

This year is going to be crazy.

This year is going to be _awesome._

I was just telling Roland about our band and he said that he knows how to play an instrument!

Really? What instrument?

The hardingfele.

Are you sure he was talking about an instrument and not some sort of weird Norwegian sport?

Pretty sure. A hardingfele is a sort of violin. Roland thinks he might be able to learn bass pretty easily because of all his hardingfele knowledge, so I'm bringing him to my lesson with Maestro Merritt.

Then Roland can be in the band! That's awesome! Can I come along, too?

What Maestro Merritt is like with Lydia

What Maestro Merritt is like with Roland

You are so lucky to have Ryan as your teacher.

goldstandard3000: Maestro Pape clearly hates me. I was telling Melody about how much he loves Roland and she said that the Maestro is probably an unenlightened woman-hater.

jladybugaboo: That could be true. Or maybe Roland is just easier to get along with?

goldstandard3000: Are you saying I'm difficult to get along with?

jladybugaboo: Noooooooooooo.

jladybugaboo: Don't you think that Papa Dad is the greatest person ever and is also very handsome and charming?

So I told my mom that Maestro
Merritt is probably a woman-hater
and it's like she didn't even hear me.

But mooooom!!!

Tra la la, ignoring Lydia!

She's so cheerful all the time.
Maybe if you practice louder, she'll
be annoyed. It seems to work
with my dads.
I've tried, but it's like she's taken
happy pills or something ever since
Melody got back. I guess she
really hated Melody's old hairstyle?

Ways to Make Maestro Merritt Like Me

① Keep bringing Roland to my lessons. If Maestro Merritt sees that Roland is in the band, he'll respect me and then he'll like me.

② Bring him a gift, like baked goods. Who wouldn't love baked goods?

③ Impress him with your dedication to learning to play the guitar.

Easy for you to say, your lessons are super-fun.

Hit that with a stick! Excellent! You're a genius!

It's a little more difficult than that.

Sure it is.

Did I see you talking with Chuck in the hallway before class?

Roland told him about the band, and he wanted to know more.

I thought he wasn't talking to you because it made Jane mad.

That's what I thought, too.

So tell me about this band...

jladybugaboo: I wonder who dumped who.

goldstandard3000: Does it matter?

jladybugaboo: Well, if Chuck dumped Jane, then he probably dumped her so he could hang out with you more, right?

goldstandard3000: He should have done that last year instead of telling me that we couldn't talk anymore.

jladybugaboo: I thought you'd be more excited about being friends with Chuck again.

goldstandard3000: It's not that simple.

jladybugaboo: What's complicated about it?

My Class Schedule and the Amount of Times I Ran into Chuck Today

1st Period— Social Studies

2nd Period— Math
Chuck said hi to me after class.

3rd Period— Study Hall

4th Period — English

5th Period— Gym
Chuck came to my locker and gave me a mix CD he made to inspire my guitar playing.

6th Period— Lunch

7th Period— French
Chuck asked me "Ça va?" after class.

8th Period— Chorus

9th Period— Science
Chuck walked me to the bus and talked about the karate class he thinks we should take together.
HE'S EVERYWHERE.

Chuck gave me another mix CD today!

That's nice. Can I see it?

It is **NOT NICE.** We have to find ways to get him off my back.

Why does he bother you? You guys used to be friends.

That was before he dated Jane.

Yeah, but he's not dating Jane anymore.

He's still the guy who stopped talking to me when he got a girlfriend. Real friends don't do that.

I think you actually might have a point.

What do you mean, "actually"?

HOW TO GET A BOY TO STOP TALKING TO YOU

1. Ignore him.

2. Hide from him.

3. Pretend to have another boyfriend. Maybe Roland? He's a **terrible** liar.

So I asked my dads how to make a boy leave you alone.

Why do you ask? Is there a boy bothering you?

What is he saying? Is he making you uncomfortable?

Dads! It's no one.

A boy keeps talking to Lydia and she's not interested.

That is ADORABLE.

I'm telling you, the blue hair is really working for her.

This is so cute, I have to call Elaine.

So they were no help and I think they're going to call your mom.
What???

Lydia, just know that if you don't want to talk to a boy, you don't have to.

You are in charge of your own personhood.

If he keeps bothering you, let me know.

But you know you can handle it. In many cultures you are considered an adult.

Okay, Mel, that's enough.

Mom, we can't crush the growing flower of Lydia's womanhood.

If I have to hear about my womanhood again, I'm going to lose it. I'll just try to avoid Chuck.

Lunch today was strange and awkward.

So I'm really sorry I was such a wackadoo last year, I was just going through stuff, you know, and I had to deal with Chuck, you know, and I'm not blaming him for my wackiness, but it was kind of his fault, so I'm sorry, okay?

I forgive you.

Thanks... who are you again?

So... We're friends with Jane again?
I don't think we have much of a choice.

goldstandard3000: Are you online?

jladybugaboo: Yes. What's up?

goldstandard3000: Jane called me and won't get off the phone.

jladybugaboo: Are you talking to her right now?

goldstandard3000: She's doing most of the talking.

jladybugaboo: What is she talking about?

goldstandard3000: Chuck. She doesn't like him. A lot.

jladybugaboo: How long has she been on the phone with you?

goldstandard3000: An hour and a half. Could you call me and then I'll pretend it's my dying grandmother or something so I can get off the phone?

So my bubbe is on the other line and she's been under the weather, so I have to go... yeah, like now.

On the one hand, being friends with Jane again is nice because it means that Gretchen can be friends with us again.

On the other hand, we haven't been able to eat lunch without Jane for the past two weeks, and she's kind of repetitive.

Hi!

Hi! Hi!

Hi!

And he never wanted to do anything, and I'd always be like, Let's do something, and he'd be all, What do you want to do, and I'd say, You're the guy, it's your job to figure it out, and he'd be all, How am I supp[ose] Uh huh [a]nd it was so annoying, yo[u]... [why] should I have to tell him w[ha]t... not my pro[blem] because se[riously] Chuck is a b...

Did you tell Jane about our band?

Why?

Because now she wants to be in the band, that's why.

Does she play an instrument?

No! All she does is sing! And we already have a singer! Why did you even tell her about the band?

I panicked! She was talking about Chuck again and I was afraid that if I didn't change the subject she'd never stop talking about the breakup and then I would COMPLETELY LOSE MY MIND. So I started talking about the band. I'm sorry.

Well, the damage is done. How are we going to tell her she's not in the band without hurting her feelings?

Jane keeps hinting about wanting to be in the band. All the time.

Bands are cool. I wish I could be in one. It's a shame that I'm not, because Mama had a soundproof room put in our basement so I could practice my singing and it's perfect for rehearsing. If I was in a band.

We've been trying to distract her every time she mentions it, but it's hard.

So when do you guys rehearse?

Hey look, a funny bird!

I think it's a plastic bag stuck in a tree. So anyway, what's your rehearsal schedule?

Just got a note from Lisa.

Meet us under the stairwell after school. Bring Lydia. Don't tell Jane!!!

What do you think that's all about?

I think we have to let Jane in the band.

What if she tries to take over everything?

She might, but we owe Lisa for covering up all the nasty graffiti about us last year, and she really wants us to let Jane in the band. Plus, I think that Papa Dad and Daddy wouldn't mind if we found somewhere else to practice.

OFFICIAL BAND MEETING
I think we should invite Jane to join the band because she really wants it and she's our friend and we can rehearse at her house.
I think it's a bad idea because she'll want to be the lead singer and that's my job.
The more, the happier! Let's let her in.
So Jane's in the band.

jladybugaboo: Did you tell Jane that she's in the band yet?

goldstandard3000: I'm about to call her. I don't know why I have to be the one to tell her.

jladybugaboo: Because it's the lead singer's job to lead.

goldstandard3000: I don't even want her in the band!

jladybugaboo: The vote was two to one.

goldstandard3000: It wasn't exactly a fair vote. You know that Roland always does whatever you want him to do.

jladybugaboo: That's not true!

goldstandard3000: Name one thing you've asked him to do that he hasn't done.

goldstandard3000: I'm waiting.

goldstandard3000: Getting old here.

goldstandard3000: I think a spider has made a cobweb in my hair.

jladybugaboo: Just call Jane!

So Jane's pretty psyched about being in the band.

This is going to be so awesome! I can't wait for rehearsal!

It's nice to see her happy.

And she hasn't mentioned Chuck in 24 hours, so that's nice.

Tomorrow is our first rehearsal at Jane's house. Not only does she have a sound proof room in her basement, but she told Roland that she also has recording equipment.

Why does she have recording equipment in her basement?

Her mother used to record her and send demo tapes to famous music producers.

That's crazy pants.

I don't know. If my mother had done that, I might have kept up with my harding fele practice.

Jane's house is kind of...
Totally nuts.
I don't think there was one wall that wasn't covered in pictures of Jane.

After our Tour de Jane's Face, we set up our instruments in the basement. Mrs. Astley would not leave us alone.

Can I get you anything? Something to drink? Snacks? There's ice cream!

Mom, stop being such a freak and get out of here!

My mom would have killed me if I said anything like that to her. I'd never talk like that to my dads! And also, I would have enjoyed some ice cream.

HOW WE SPENT OUR FIRST REHEARSAL AT JANE'S HOUSE

It wasn't the most productive day.

CREATIVE DECISION MAKING
Figuring out what sort of music to play was harder than we thought it would be.
We're a rock band. We should play rock music.
What kind? There are a lot of different kinds.
I don't know, music that rocks.
We should do more vocal-based stuff, you know, because we have two singers.
We should probably play something easy because we're not very good.
I'm good at singing.
Um, okay.

We decided to think it over and make a decision later. Then we made a list of possible band names.

The Dragonflies — ☑ Lydia's idea

The Outcasts — ☑ Roland's idea

The Broken Hipsters — ☑ Jane's idea

Mischief and Mayhem — ☐ My (Julie's) idea

Mayhem Soufflé

Humanity Salad

Omkjøring

Forskjellig

Winner!

(The Macramé Owls)

3 Girls and a Norwegian

Welcome to My Face

The Dinks

Noodle butt

It's so ugly, it's cool.

It might be so ugly that it's really ugly.

Somehow the word about the Macramé Owls has gotten out— everyone is talking about it.

Gig: A live performance by a musician or a group playing popular music

Did Jane mention any details? Like where we'll be playing, who we'll be playing for, that sort of thing?

I think she said that she'd tell us after school, but it was like I heard her through a tunnel. I was focusing on not passing out or barfing or screaming and running away in terror.

This could be a really big opportunity.

This could be a HUGE NIGHTMARE.

What's the point of being in a band if we don't play for people?

WE DON'T KNOW HOW TO PLAY A SINGLE SONG!!!

Okay, so my mom is best friends with Kate, and Kate has a daughter named Brittany, and when Kate heard that I was in a band she asked my mom if she could hire us to play at Brittany's birthday party!
Do we know Brittany?
She doesn't go to our school.
Why would she want us to play at the party if she's never heard us?
Kate's heard me sing before and she knows I'm good, so I guess that was enough.

It's perfect! We'll get some experience playing in front of people and if it doesn't go so great it won't matter because we don't know anyone.

WE DON'T KNOW HOW TO PLAY ANYTHING

So we'll practice more. The party isn't for another three weeks! That should be enough time to write and learn a bunch of songs. We'll brainstorm during our next rehearsal.

Gross!

I told Ryan about THE GIG and he seemed to think that it was a pretty good opportunity.

But he promised that if I practiced a lot I might be ready by Brittany's party. Actually, he said "readyish."

jladybugaboo: Is it weird that we're performing for the first time for a person that we don't know at all who has never heard us play?

goldstandard3000: By the time we're done, Brittany will know us and love us and want to hear us play again, and that won't be weird at all.

jladybugaboo: How can you be so confident that she'll like our music? I'm not so confident that I like our music. Actually, I'm not so confident that you can call the sounds that we make with our instruments "music" yet.

goldstandard3000: I have a plan.

jladybugaboo: Oh! Goody. The four most terrifying words in the universe.

goldstandard3000: Hush. I figure that if we find out more about Brittany, we can write a song especially for her, and then even if it doesn't sound exactly amazing, she'll still be happy with it.

jladybugaboo: That's actually not a terrible plan.

goldstandard3000: What do you mean, "actually"?

We asked Jane what Brittany was like, and her answers were weird.

I don't know her very well. I think she likes unicorns. And rainbows, she definitely likes rainbows. And frosting.

Frosting?

Um, yeah.

Well, who doesn't like frosting?

I do not know how we're supposed to make this into a song.

Song for Brittany
by Lydia Goldblatt and
Julie Graham-Chang

UNICORNS!!!
Look out for the Unicorns!
They are large and have
sharp horns!

UNICORNS!!!

UNICORNS!!!
Rainbows are their magic streets!
Frosting is what they like to eats!
UNICORNS!!!

UNICORNS!!!
Run away, they have dangerous
weapons on their heads!
If you stay you will soon be dead!
UNICORNS!!!

Do you think it
might be too dark?
It's funny! Brittany
will love it.

NEW SONG!

I just saw Jamie Burke chewing
on a book.
Jamie might be the world's
worst cook.

Jamie once tried to fly to the moon.
He jumped off a roof while
holding a balloon.

Jamie does things you can't explain.
He once tried to chase a
speeding train.

Jamie made a sculpture of
old chewed-up gum.
And tried to sell it for a
tidy sum.

Jamie Burke! Jamie Burke!
You really love to eat
homework!

Jamie Burke! Jamie Burke!
Something something rhymes
with Burke!

This one might need
a little more work.

84

We've written seven original songs!
Putting them to music was pretty easy.

Maybe it was easy because every song sounds the same, and by "the same," I mean <u>bad.</u>

The songs could use some tweaking.

goldstandard3000: I played the Unicorn Song to Maestro Merritt during my lesson and he didn't totally hate it!

jladybugaboo: Really? What did he say?

goldstandard3000: He said, "I don't totally hate it."

jladybugaboo: Wow, that's great!

goldstandard3000: I know! He told me that while it was a pretty bad song, he could tell that I worked really hard on it, and that he was pleased with the way that the calluses are forming on my fingers.

jladybugaboo: That's gross and fantastic!

goldstandard3000: I know! It just makes me want to practice harder. And maybe write better songs.

jladybugaboo: One thing at a time.

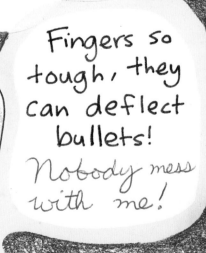

Fingers so tough, they can deflect bullets! Nobody mess with me!

A FUNNY THING THAT HAPPENED AT REHEARSAL

(and by "funny," you mean *TERRIBLE*)

I brought snackies! And I have a few teensy questions. Do you plan to play so loud at the party? Kate might not like that. And she needs to know what songs you plan to play, so I'll need you to make a list...

MOM, GET OUT, WE'RE WORKING.

So I gave her our song list, she left for about ten minutes, and then returned to give it back to me.

~~Jamie Burke Eats Homework~~

Song for Brittany

~~Talk to My Katana~~

~~Alien Invasion~~

~~Chuck Your Boyfriend~~

~~Drama Drama Drama Drama~~

~~Skal vi danse?~~

LIST OF REJECTED SONGS

~~Some suggestions for~~ more appropriate songs

Happy Birthday

The Wheels on the Bus

I'm a Little Teapot

The Itsy Bitsy Spider

So apparently Brittany doesn't go to our school because she's **6**.

Actually, she's five. She's turning six.

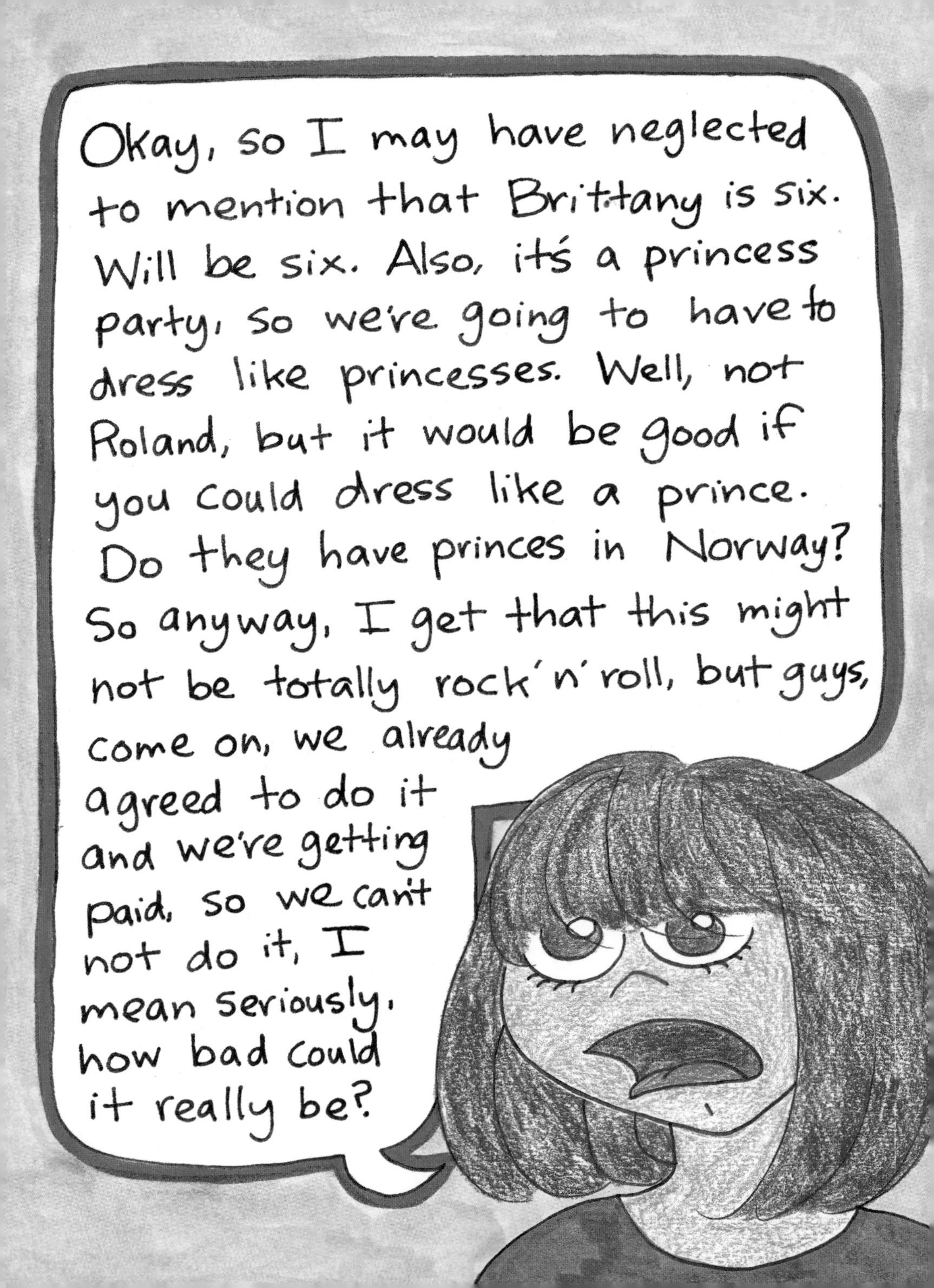
Okay, so I may have neglected to mention that Brittany is six. Will be six. Also, it's a princess party, so we're going to have to dress like princesses. Well, not Roland, but it would be good if you could dress like a prince. Do they have princes in Norway? So anyway, I get that this might not be totally rock'n'roll, but guys, come on, we already agreed to do it and we're getting paid, so we can't not do it, I mean seriously, how bad could it really be?

We were so mad at Jane, but the problem with being mad at someone when you rehearse at her house is that you can't just storm out (particularly when you have to wait for your dad to pick you up because you can't just leave your drum set).

I thought you did a really good job of angrily packing up the car.

It took a lot of energy.

goldstandard3000: Has Jane tried to call you?

jladybugaboo: Yes. FOUR TIMES.

goldstandard3000: She's called me five times. I think she's going to keep calling until we agree to play the party.

jladybugaboo: She should have told us.

goldstandard3000: What are we going to do?

jladybugaboo: What do you mean, what are we going to do?

goldstandard3000: Well, it is a paying gig. And there's a little girl who expects us to be there.

jladybugaboo: I. Am. Not. Dressing. Up. Like. A. Princess.

So we talked to a few people about our "princess situation."

Well, if you promised to do it, you have to do it.

Bwah ha!

Maybe it will be fun?

Teaching to worship monarchy encourages classism.

Roland was not in a talking mood.

I don't know why you're upset. "The Wheels on the Bus" could be a rocking tune.

Jen might be onto something.

OUR PARTY PLAN

We're going to play the princess party. And we're going to play the songs we're allowed to play. But...

We're going to play them <u>Our Way</u>.

Great! Thank you, thank you! Only... What is "Our Way"?

We're not entirely sure yet.

I am not dressing up like a prince.

And Roland won't be dressing up like a prince.

We've got three days to figure out what "our way" is, and right now the only thing we know is that the songs shouldn't sound like kiddie songs usually sound, mostly because we don't really know how to play them on our instruments.

Certainly not in a way that would be recognizable to human ears.

This sounds like music to me!

It is a good thing that we are not humans, for if we were, this would sound pretty terrible.

Thank goodness we're aliens. Let us dance!

It's a little weird that Jane wanted us to play this princess party, and yet she's the one who really turned the songs into something... different.

Something... screamy.

She seemed a little angry.
a little?

Is it just me, or are we starting to sound awesome?

It may be just you.

You are so funny!

At first I thought Jane was just trying to hog the spotlight, but she was really, really into it.

She's very good at screaming a lot.

Listening to her hurt my throat.

Thank goodness for soundproofing.

OFFICIAL BAND OUTFITS
Rainbow colors
Paper crowns
Glitter everywhere

The party is TOMORROW

jladybugaboo: Are you nervous?

goldstandard3000: Kind of. But then I remember that we're playing for a bunch of six-year-olds.

jladybugaboo: But what if they don't like us?

goldstandard3000: Why wouldn't they like us? We'll be covered in glitter. Six-year-olds love that.

jladybugaboo: But what if they don't like our music?

goldstandard3000: They'll be all hyped up on cake and ice cream. They'd probably be excited about the mail arriving. Besides, we're older and cool-looking. They won't care about our music at all. And even if they hate it, what are they going to do?

What 6-Year-Olds Do When They Don't Like Your Music

It wasn't that bad.
IT WAS **WORSE**.
It was much worse.

At first things weren't so bad. We got to the party, and while we were setting up the kids were really interested in us.

What are you doing?

We're setting up our instruments.

Why?

So we can play music.

Why?

Because it's your birthday.

Why?

Because you were born six years ago.

Why?

That went on for a while.

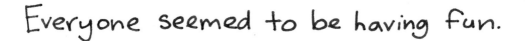

Everyone seemed to be having fun.

Remember when we used to have huge birthday parties with cake and party favors and games?

It's so lame that we're too cool for that sort of thing now.

Being cool is hard.

And then...we began to play.

Brittany's Mom

Jane's Mom

The Princesses

WHEELS ON THE BUS

And then things got ugly.

We had to hide in the garage until Mrs. Asbjørnsen came to pick us up.

I'm going to have nightmares about princesses. They're so bitey!

I'm going to have nightmares about Jane's mom.

I have never been more embarrassed in my entire life. I allowed you to spend time with these people and this is how you repay me?

What did she mean, "These people"?

I'm really proud of you guys for defying traditional expectations and subverting the power structure.

Does "subverting the power structure" mean "not getting paid"?

You don't need money if you're rich in noble principles.

Will noble principles buy me a skein of yarn?

One day you'll understand.

I miss old cranky Melody. New hippie Melody is annoying.

goldstandard3000: Has Jane called you?

jladybugaboo: Nope. You?

goldstandard3000: No. It's weird not getting constant calls from her.

jladybugaboo: Do you think she's grounded?

goldstandard3000: She's probably not eating cake.

jladybugaboo: I can't believe we didn't even get any cake at the party.

goldstandard3000: And I think the cake was supposed to be our payment.

jladybugaboo: Seriously? That's stingy.

goldstandard3000: And I think it had strawberries in it, so you would have had an allergic reaction anyway.

jladybugaboo: I can't believe we didn't even get paid the worst payment ever.

goldstandard3000: And I still have glitter in my hair.

jladybugaboo: Me, too.

We're never using glitter again.

Have you seen Jane yet?

No. How's she doing?

She's different.

What do you mean?

You should probably see for yourself.

I can't believe Jane dyed her hair blue. That's _my_ thing!

What are you going to do?

I don't know! Should I dye my hair purple?

What if she dyes her hair purple?

This is a nightmare!

Everyone is talking about Jane's hair

She looks like you, Lydia!

I heard that her mom screamed until she passed out.

Did you know that Jane is in a rock band?

I heard that they're amazing!

Unbelievable.

And now everyone is talking about the Princess Party gig.

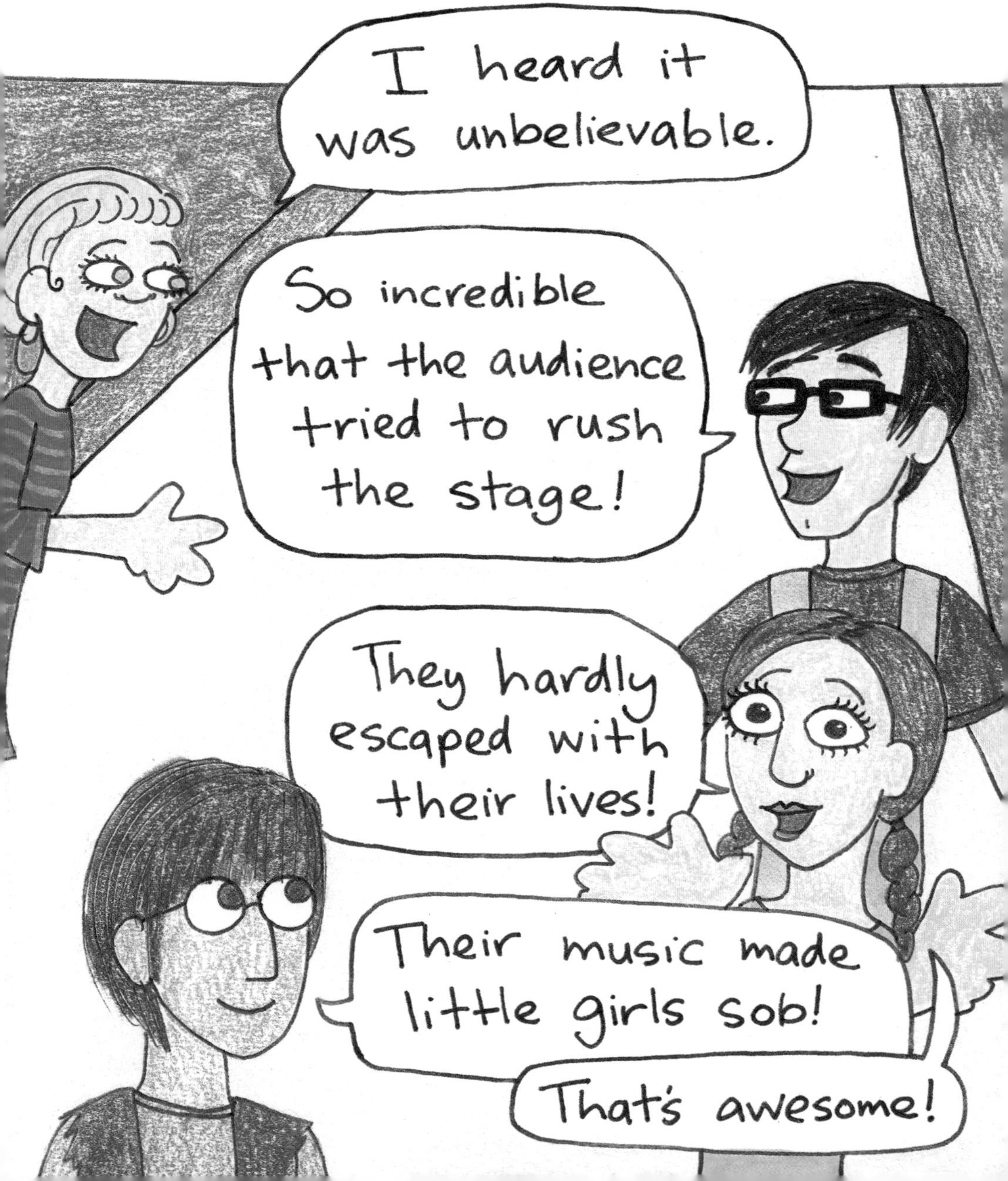

We have to call a band meeting. Things are getting crazy.

How can we have a band meeting if Jane is grounded?

How can Jane go to the mall and buy hair dye if she's grounded? I don't think Jane's mom knows what grounding means.

So you think she can come to a meeting?

Probably. Can we have it at your house?

Why my house?

You have the heaviest instrument.

Oh. You want to practice here again?

We missed you. A lot. Really.

goldstandard3000: Is Jane coming the band meeting tomorrow?

jladybugaboo: Yes. I think she's telling her mom that we're working on a report or something.

goldstandard3000: My mom would see through that in a second.

jladybugaboo: Papa Dad would be all, "Oh, what's your report on…LYING???"

goldstandard3000: Ha! He would totally do that. Is her mom completely stupid?

jladybugaboo: Jane seems to think she is. Are you going to talk to Jane about her hair?

goldstandard3000: I don't know. What would I say? If I ask her why she copied me, it will look like I'm jealous because her blue hair is cooler than my blue hair. Besides, it's a free country, she can do what she wants to do.

jladybugaboo: I think your blue hair is cooler.

goldstandard3000: You have to say that, you're my best friend.

jladybugaboo: True, but I think yours is cooler because you did it first.

Places to Play Where We Won't Be Attacked by Small Children with Sharp Teeth

1. SCHOOL AUDITORIUM

Problem: We're probably not allowed.

② AWESOME ROCK CLUB

Problem: We don't actually know where any awesome rock clubs are.

Actually, we don't know where any rock clubs are, regardless of whether or not they are awesome.

And we're probably still too young to get into them even if we knew where they were.

3. A PARTY THAT ISN'T FOR SIX-YEAR-OLDS

Problem: We don't get invited to parties.

Why is that? We used to get invited to parties all the time.

We used to be six.

Playing at a party is probably the best thing to do, but now we need to find a party, and we don't even know what non-Princess Tea Party parties are like.

We could find out.

How?

Research.

MISSION: FIND A PARTY

We have to start observing again so we can figure out where good parties are.

Or any parties.

Maybe if we go to one party, while we're there we'll hear about another party, and then we'll be known as the band that goes to parties, and that will lead us to being the band that plays at parties.

We just have to find that first party.

So what's this I hear about a party? Oh, you weren't talking about a party? If you happen to start talking about a party, could you maybe mention the date and address?

goldstandard3000: Any luck today?

jladybugaboo: No. I think I heard Senora Weinstein talking with Madame Chiger about a party, but I think that might be overshooting our age range. Did you hear about anything?

goldstandard3000: Sort of.

jladybugaboo: Really? Where?

goldstandard3000: I heard Melody talking on the phone about going to a party this weekend.

jladybugaboo: We can't go to a high school party.

goldstandard3000: Sure we can. Why not?

jladybugaboo: Everyone will be very big. And old. And scary. And big.

goldstandard3000: I think we can go. We just have to be prepared.

jladybugaboo: For what?

Big, old, scary, and big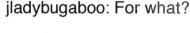

High school parties are different from junior high parties, so we need a game plan before going to one.

How can you say that a high school party is different from a junior high party when you've never been to either?

A high school party has to be different! First of all, we won't know anyone.

ADVANTAGES OF NOT KNOWING ANYONE AT A PARTY

1. We don't have to tell anyone that we're only 13.
2. We don't have to tell anyone our real names.
3. We don't have to worry about looking cool because we don't have to see anyone at school afterward.
4. I can use the British accent that took six months to learn.

Oh god. I'll give you a dollar not to.

I've made us code names for the party. What do you think?
CODE NAMES
Lydia:
Lillian Gold
Julie:
Juliet Chang-Graham
Roland:
Rodney Smith
Are you serious?
Oooh, can I be Wilhelmina Spicehandler?

goldstandard3000: The party is tomorrow—do you know what you're going to wear?

jladybugaboo: I don't even know if I'm going.

goldstandard3000: Come on, what's the worst thing that could happen?

jladybugaboo: Oh, I don't know. Our parents could find out that we're going to a high school party and kill us, or maybe they won't have to because the high school kids will find out that we're in junior high and they'll kill us.

goldstandard3000: I don't think that's what high school kids usually do.

jladybugaboo: Oh, but you don't know, do you? YOU DON'T KNOW ANYTHING BECAUSE NO JUNIOR HIGH KID HAS EVER GONE TO A HIGH SCHOOL PARTY AND LIVED TO TELL THE TALE.

goldstandard3000: Do you feel better now that you got that out of your system?

jladybugaboo: A little.

goldstandard3000: Good. I think we should probably wear jeans and sneakers, just in case we might need to make a run for it if things don't go well.

jladybugaboo: WHAT???

goldstandard3000: KIDDING! Just kidding. Still, wear sneakers.

THE PARTY PLAN

The party is near Jen's house, so we're going to tell our parents that we're sleeping over at her place, which is true. What we're not going to tell our parents is that we're going to meet up with Roland and walk over to the party.

Jane can't come because she's still grounded.

Rules of Party Conduct

① When at this party, we will NOT be using code names because they're confusing and weird.

② If offered cigarettes, alcohol, or ANYTHING, we will politely refuse.
What if they offer us cookies? REFUSE.

③ NO FAKE ACCENTS.

④ Our safety word is "noodle," and if at any time one of us says, "noodle," that means we should all run away immediately.

NOODLE!!

Where are you girls headed?
We're meeting up with a boy and then going to a party with older kids so we can collect data on what a cool party is like.
Don't drink anything and be back by 1Ø.
Yes, Mom.
Yes, Dr. Mattocks.

I'm not exactly sure what we were expecting to find at the party —

But we were not expecting what we found —

Uh... who are you?

I panicked.

Hi! We're here to...help with whatever you're doing.

We are very helpful people.

Then I super-panicked.

I'm her sister!

Then it was like we'd broken the New Hippie Melody spell and freed Old Cranky Melody.

What. Are. You. Doing. HERE.

It was both nice and terrifying to see her again. Then, just as she was about to kill us until we were very, very dead, a miracle happened.

Hey, grab some chairs, we'd love the help. Mel, you never told me you had a sister.

We thought it would be such a big party that Melody wouldn't notice us, but it turned out to be just a bunch of teenagers planning to protest the food in the high school cafeteria.

Do you know what's in chicken nuggets and hot dogs? You don't want to know.

That's why I'm a vegan.

That's terrific!

So they put us to work making signs. It was fun!

Melody's friends were really nice. Melody's friends couldn't love Jen more if they tried.

Melody's friends couldn't love Jen more if she was covered in organic broccoli.

Melody's friends couldn't love Jen more if she offered them rides on a flying tofu-eating unicorn.

We were having a good time, but it wasn't completely not weird to be there.

At 9:30 we left the party and went back to Jen's house.

It's so cool that Jen's mom didn't care about us going to a high school party. She just trusts Jen.

I guess so. I wonder if we had been as honest with our parents as Jen was with her mom, they might trust us, too.

That's crazy talk, crazytalker. Talkin' crazy with your crazy mouth.

I'm going to a party with high school kids tonight!

Great! We're going with you!

Prepare to be embarrassed!

You have a point.

goldstandard3000: I think Melody's mad at me.

jladybugaboo: Is she going to tell your mom about the party? Because if she tells your mom, your mom is going to tell my dads.

goldstandard3000: I know, I know. Why do they have to be such good friends?

jladybugaboo: Did she tell your mom?

goldstandard3000: No. But she's been giving me the stinky face ever since we got back from Jen's house.

jladybugaboo: Just the stinky face? That's not so bad. She used to do that all the time and it didn't bother you.

goldstandard3000: I know, but I haven't seen her do the stinky face in months. What if she was bursting with pent-up stinky face and we released it by going to the party?

jladybugaboo: MEGA STINKY FACE.

goldstandard3000: ULTIMATE STINKY FACE.

jladybugaboo: REVENGE OF THE STINKY FACE.

goldstandard3000: I think I'll lie low for a while.

jladybugaboo: Good idea.

Have you seen Jane today?
Not yet. Did she shave her head?
No, but she wants to know everything about the party. You might want to eat your lunch before you get to the cafeteria because she is not going to let up until you've told her every detail.
It wasn't that exciting.
That's what I tried to tell her, but she didn't seem to care.

And who was there again? Was he cute? And how tall was he? And how old ᵈ you think he wᵃ Where is thᵉ party aⁿ wh my gᵒ

And then...

All of a sudden everyone knew that we'd gone to the party. People we didn't know knew who we were and knew that we'd gone to a party.

I heard you totally snuck in through the back door.

Uh...

And you guys didn't get caught?

Actually...

What did you wear?

Um... pants?

That's awesome!

What's going on?

Everyone knows we went to a party?

I know! Isn't it great?

It's weird. I just had a whole conversation with an 8th grader about it.

Which 8th grader?

I have no idea.

Did she invite you to another party?

No.

Trust me, it's only a matter of time before the invites start rolling in.

goldstandard3000: Any invites today?

jladybugaboo: Nope. You?

goldstandard3000: No. If everyone's still talking about us, I can't understand why we haven't been invited to a bunch of parties.

jladybugaboo: Maybe there aren't any parties to be invited to.

goldstandard3000: Do you really think that's it?

jladybugaboo: I don't know. But if the fact that we went to a party is big news, I guess that not too many people go to parties.

goldstandard3000: If we can't get invited to a party, we're never going to get the opportunity to play in front of anyone.

jladybugaboo: Darn it! That is disappointing.

goldstandard3000: I know, you're crushed.

jladybugaboo: My heart is broken. Really. I don't even know how I continue to breathe.

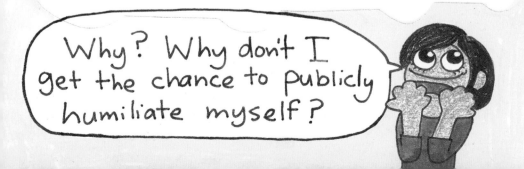

Why? Why don't I get the chance to publicly humiliate myself?

After we'd gone through all of our songs, Roland told us his idea.

I know how we can find a party.

Is your older brother Pete going to one? I would totally go to a party that he would be at.

Actually, I was thinking that we should throw a party ourselves for Lydia and Julie.

You're both teenagers now and I never got to give you presents!

Roland is some sort of GENIUS.

It's perfect because we'll only invite people who will appreciate our music, and we'll also get birthday presents!

Even though our birthdays were two months ago.

We will graciously forgive everyone for missing our birthdays as long as they enjoy our performance and buy us things.

We are nothing if not gracious.

I forgive you for forgetting my birthday!

Hooray!

goldstandard3000: I don't think that we should have the party at Roland's house.

jladybugaboo: Why not?

goldstandard3000: I think it might be too Norwegian.

jladybugaboo: How can something be too Norwegian?

goldstandard3000: It's full of troll sculptures. They're everywhere. And his mom is nice, but what if she starts offering everyone stinky Norwegian fish paste?

jladybugaboo: That would be gross and weird. So where would we have the party?

goldstandard3000: Your house?

jladybugaboo: My house? Why not your house?

WHY WE SHOULD HAVE OUR PARTY at JULIE'S HOUSE

① Julie doesn't have to worry about dealing with Melody, who currently wants to kill me.

(still mad) →

② If we have the party at Julie's house, we won't have to move her heavy drum set.

(Enormous)

③ Julie's birthday is more recent.

ADVANTAGES OF HAVING OUR PARTY at LYDIA'S HOUSE

1. Lydia's mom is currently happy all the time, and will probably be in a good mood when we ask her.

> A party? That sounds delightful! Tra la la fun!

2. Lydia's mom is not Papa Dad, and will not take every opportunity to embarrass us when the house is full of people.

> I will not mention your fear of turtles.

This is so lame. Can't we just have the party at Jane's house?

WHAT THE PARTY WOULD BE LIKE AT JANE'S HOUSE

NOW WHO WANTS A CUPCAKE?

SOMEBODY BETTER EAT THESE CUPCAKES.

Maybe we shouldn't even ask to have it at Jane's house.

You may be onto something.

goldstandard3000: Have you asked your dads yet now?

jladybugaboo: No.

goldstandard3000: Have you asked your dads yet?

jladybugaboo: NO.

goldstandard3000: How about now?

jladybugaboo: No.

goldstandard3000: And now?

jladybugaboo: No.

goldstandard3000: Seriously, when are you going to ask your dads?

jladybugaboo: I NEVER AGREED TO ASK THEM TO HAVE A PARTY!

goldstandard3000: I know! How about now?

jladybugaboo: I really can't imagine why Melody would ever be annoyed by you.

STRATEGY!

Suggestions for How to Ask Your Dads to Have a Party Two Months After Your Birthday

Just ask! The worst they can say is no.

Tell them it's a good opportunity for social interaction outside of the classroom setting.

Are you sure you don't want to have the party at my house? My mom makes wonderful tilslørte bondepiker.

I don't think that would go so well.

I'm going to ask my dads about the party today — on one condition.

Great!

THE CONDITION is that you have to come with me.

Okay. Do we have a plan?

I think I'm just going to ask them.

Sounds good. I didn't want to have to fake cry.

Do you think that would ever work with your mom?

Sure. When pigs fly.

Then they went away to DISCUSS.

DADDY AND PAPA DAD'S
RULES FOR PARTYING

1. We have to set up the house (put away all things breakable, valuable, stainable, and perishable).

2. No more than 20 people.

3. The party will have a clear starting and ending time.

4. The dads reserve the right to throw people out or end the party if they don't like what's going on.

5. We have to clean the inside of their car.

I've made up invitations and we're each going to hand them out to five people.

Come and Celebrate
Lydia and Julie's Birthdays
with a Special Performance by

The
MACRAMÉ
OWLS!

LIVE IN CONCERT!
October 25th, from 7 to 10pm
28 Goodwin Road

Looks great!

Did you hand out your five invites yet?

I gave my invites to Jen, Maxine, Deirdre, Lisa, and Jamie.

You didn't give one to Gretchen?

I figured Jane would give one of hers to Gretchen.

I was going to give one of mine to Gretchen. Wait, you gave one to Jamie Burke???

I thought he'd like to hear his song. Also we could probably use some boys at the party.

Isn't it Roland's job to invite the boys?

What boys does he know? He's always hanging out with us.

jladybugaboo: Did you invite Mike Cavelleri to the party?

goldstandard3000: No. Why?

jladybugaboo: He told me today that he was looking forward to coming.

goldstandard3000: Maybe Jane invited him?

jladybugaboo: It's weird that she'd invite him if she's still angry with his brother. She's still angry with Chuck, right?

goldstandard3000: I'm pretty sure she still is. Maybe Roland invited him.

jladybugaboo: I had no idea they were even friends.

goldstandard3000: Maybe Roland is a MAN OF MYSTERY with SECRET FRIENDSHIPS.

jladybugaboo: That's a laugh. Roland can't keep secrets to save his life.

goldstandard3000: I don't know. I bet he's got a surprise or two up his sleeve.

WE HAVE A PROBLEM.

Is it that our party is in four days and we aren't very good at playing music?

No. **ROLAND INVITED CHUCK TO THE PARTY.**

Oh no. Why did he do that?

Chuck is my friend.

Didn't it ever occur to you that "Chuck Your Boyfriend" is about him?

You know, that song makes a lot more sense now.

Jane is going to completely lose her mind.

HOW TO EXPLAIN THE CHUCK SITUATION TO JANE

① We just tell her.

Roland invited Chuck to the party.

I WILL NOW LOSE MY MIND!

② We tell her on the phone.

Roland invited Chuck to the party.

MIND GONE NOW! BLOR! BLAAARG.!!!

We ended up telling Jane about Chuck's invite during rehearsal. She was sort of okay with it.

Why would I mind? I don't care if he's invited. He should be invited. No. PROBLEM.

Her voice was a little high-pitched.

I think it hurt Bad Cat's ears.

MROOW!

Stuff to Prepare for the Party

First we have to hide everything in the house that is breakable, valuable, stainable, or perishable.

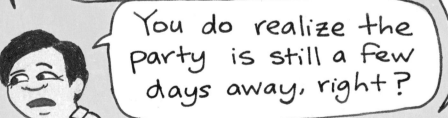

Totally psyched for the party, Jules.

An eighth grader just told me that she was excited about our party.

Really? Which eighth grader?

I don't even know! And her friend seemed to know about the party, too. How many people did Jane and Roland invite?

Don't worry, we only printed out twenty invitations. They could only invite five each.

I don't know if I like the idea of random weirdos in my house.

If they're friends of Jane, I'm sure they're okay.

What makes you so sure?

A VERY STRANGE COMMENT THAT JEN MADE TODAY

It's pretty cool that you guys aren't nervous about playing in front of so many people.

What did she mean, "So many people"?

Oh my god oh my god Jen showed us THIS.

Come and Celebrate
Lydia and Julie's Birthdays
with a Special Performance by
The
MACRAMÉ OWLS!
LIVE IN CONCERT!
October 25th, from 7 to 10 pm
28 Goodwin Road

We made color invites! Who made these?

POSSIBLE SUSPECTS

1. Evil Photocopier Imp
(a horrible creature who misuses photocopy machines)

Wheeee! I'm evil.

2. A Possessed Photocopy Machine

Must. Make. Copies. Of. Invitation.

3. JANE.

WHAT ARE WE GOING TO DO?

We are going to remain calm.
We are not going to freak out.
TOO LATE. We don't even
know who got the invitation.
Criminal psychopaths could be
coming to my house!!!!!!!!
That seems kind of unlikely.

I think Julie might be losing her mind.

It's the end of the world! We need to hide! We need to throw up! aaaaAHHH!!!

But we need to keep calm about this. Lots of people might have invitations, but that doesn't mean that lots of people will actually show up.

We should cancel the party.

How? We wouldn't even know who to call to tell its been canceled.

Can't we make an announcement or something?

Here ye, hear ye, don't come to my party!

jladybugaboo: We have to tell my dads that there are going to be more than 20 people at the party.

goldstandard3000: Why? We don't even know if there are going to be more than 20 people. It might just end up being you, me, Roland, Jane, Jen, and maybe those two eighth graders, and then you would have worried your dads for no reason.

jladybugaboo: They are going to freak out if it's more than 20 people!

goldstandard3000: Will they even notice? What are they going to do, count heads?

jladybugaboo: Maybe. Papa Dad is really tall. He can probably count 20 people in a room.

goldstandard3000: Stop it. It's going to be okay. If there are more than 20 people, and your dads don't like it, we can make some people leave.

jladybugaboo: How?

goldstandard3000: We can introduce them to Bad Cat?

THE PARTY IS **TONIGHT.** So far we've cleaned the house, set up the instruments, put out two bowls of nacho chips and a platter of veggies (Daddy insisted), plastic cups, and soda.

Now all we have to do is wait. This is the worst feeling in the world.

So far only Roland has arrived. He brought us presents and now Papa Dad is making him say things in Norwegian.

Still no Jane. And no one else. Yet.

Hvor et Jane?

Jeg forstår ikke.

Gratulerer, Julie!

If she's not here in five minutes, I'm going to freak out.

7:00

No Jane, no one else, and now Papa Dad thinks he's fluent in Norwegian.

Hvor kan jag få tak i en fiske som snakker engelsk?

I can't believe no one came. I bet you're happy now.

Well, I didn't want no one to come. I'm probably more bummed than relieved, if it helps any.

It helps a little.

Stuff That Could Have Happened to Jane

1.) Her mother found out about the party and grounded her for real.

2.) Her dad felt bad and took her on a vacation to the Caribbean.

3.) She couldn't stand the thought of seeing Chuck so she bailed on us.

4.) She freaked out about playing in front of everyone and ran away.

 you freaked out at me.

And you yelled at me.

WHY DID I EVER AGREE TO ANY OF THIS?

BECAUSE YOU WANTED TO SHOW PEOPLE YOU COULD BE MORE THAN A SHORT GIRL WHO GETS BOSSED AROUND.

You were right.
I know.
Don't let it go to your head.
Too late!
I can't believe you called me short.

At  Jane finally showed up.

Where were you?!?

Well, I couldn't just show up on time, could I? I had to make an entrance. Chuck can't think that I was just waiting around for him — that's crazy!

That's crazy?

WHAT ARE you WEARING???

And then the house really started to fill up.

People were starting to stare, so we hid out in the bathroom. That's when things went downhill fast. You were the first to lose it.
Again.

There are too many people... can't breath... oh my god...

And then you began to yell at Jane...

WHY ARE YOU DRESSED LIKE YOU'RE ON A RED CARPET? THIS IS SO NOT ROCK AND ROLL!

And then we all completely lost it.

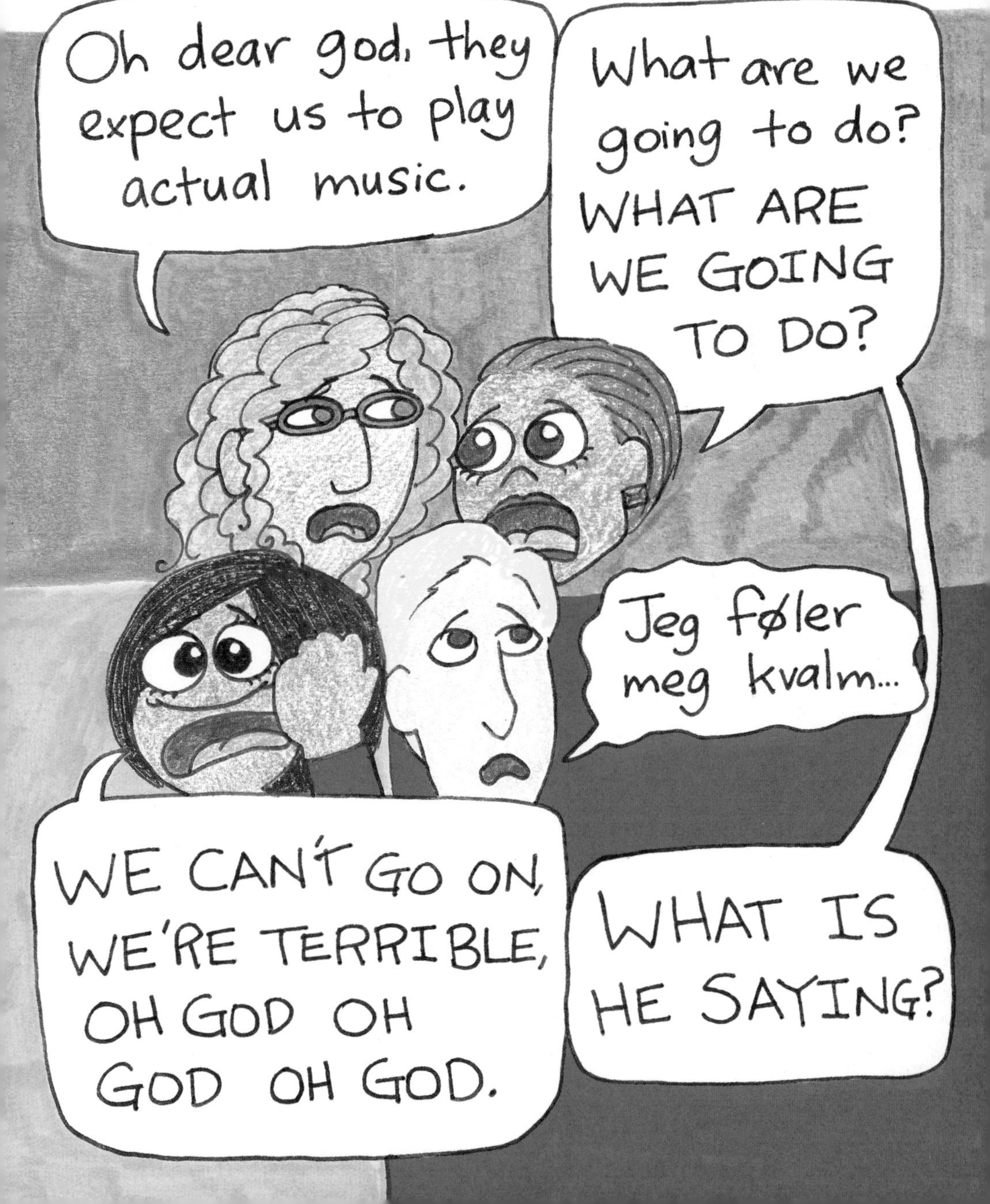

Come out already. Everyone is waiting to hear you play.

We can't! Julie is about to pass out and Roland has forgotten how to speak English and Jane looks like a Christmas tree ornament and WE SOUND TERRIBLE.

Jeg har kuldegysninger...

And then Melody told us something very interesting.

I can't believe that Melody's advice actually worked.

Okay, calm down, everyone breathe. I've been to a few house parties with bands, and all you need to do is play so loud that no one can talk over the music to point out how terrible you are.

It totally worked!

191

I am saying something to you but you can't hear me!
I don't know what you're saying but I assume you think this music is awesome!
I am smiling!
So am I!
This is great!
What? I can't hear you over this great music!

By our third song people were screaming and dancing and sweating.

It was awesome.

And terrifying.

Completely terrifying.

That's when my dads stepped in.

That was great!

But now the music part of the party is over. Who wants to play charades?

A nice, extremely quiet game of charades.

They were so embarrassing. Thank goodness.

After almost everyone left the party, the people who stayed just hung out and we began to play music.

Who knew that Jen could play guitar?

Not terrible at all.

So what's up with the Roland cuddles? Nothing! I may have mentioned that I was cold. Shut up.

I have to admit, everything was so much better when people left. After Roland calmed down enough to start speaking English again, he gave me my birthday present.

They're the same pants that were worn by the Norwegian Olympic Curling Team!

Umm... Takk!

They're pretty hideous, but I might as well wear them to school tomorrow. Everyone's going to think we're losers for having our party shut down.

I dare you to wear them.

jladybugaboo: Can you sleep?

goldstandard3000: Yes. I am sleeping and typing. SLEEPTYPING.

jladybugaboo: Are you nervous about going to school tomorrow?

goldstandard3000: A little. Mel told me that everything was going to be fine, but you know, she's crazy.

jladybugaboo: But is she? I thought her advice was actually pretty good.

goldstandard3000: Ugh, stop making a valid point, you're totally ruining my ability to make fun of Baldilocks.

jladybugaboo: What do you think really happened to her in Guatemala?

goldstandard3000: She got some sun and shaved her head.

jladybugaboo: Do you think that you can just decide to be a different person?

goldstandard3000: No. But I think you can always try to be a better person.

jladybugaboo: I like that.

goldstandard3000: I'm very wise.

jladybugaboo: Go to sleep, Yoda.

I just overheard two eighth graders talking about our party!

What were they saying?

Are you serious? We sounded like drowning cats!

I know!

Overheard in the halls of Hannibal Hamlin JUNIOR HIGH

So amazing. They're going to be famous one day, definitely.

Poor Julia, her dads are so lame.

I thought her name was Juliet?

Did you see Lydia's pants today?

So cool, I have to get a pair.

Maybe my pants are actually cool? I don't know. I looked at them this morning and now I'm blind.

Lunch today was crazy.

Oh my god, everyone loves us, we have to get more gigs, we need a publicist, oh look, there's Chuck! Hi muffin!

Hi honey.

Are you kidding me ???

goldstandard3000: I can't believe that Jane and Chuck are back together.

jladybugaboo: I'm still kind of surprise that they were ever together in the first place.

goldstandard3000: But seriously. SERIOUSLY. She wrote a song called "Chuck Your Boyfriend"! He wanted to break up with her for months. They made each other miserable! WHY ARE THEY BACK TOGETHER???

jladybugaboo: Why do you even care? You didn't even want to be friends with him again after he chose her over you.

goldstandard3000: I don't care! I just don't understand it.

jladybugaboo: Romance is mysterious.

goldstandard3000: You would know.

jladybugaboo: What do you mean?

goldstandard3000: I saw you and Roland at the party.

jladybugaboo: We just cuddled a little. What did you see?

WHAT "JUST CUDDLED A LITTLE" LOOKS LIKE

Oh my god, you saw that?!? Who else saw that???

Just me.

Okay, so Roland sort of kissed me. He gave me my birthday present and it was a really nice bracelet and we were both so relieved that we'd made it through the show without anyone booing us, and then he kind of leaned in and kissed me and now he thinks he's my boyfriend and I don't know what to do.

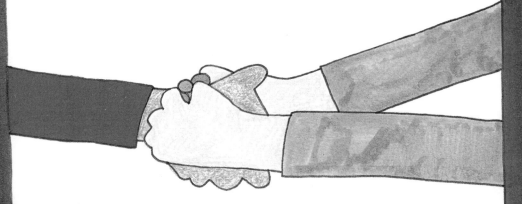

Well, is he your boyfriend or not?

I don't know...

goldstandard3000: New song idea! We can call it "A Norwegian Kissed Me."

jladybugaboo: I am not doing this.

goldstandard3000: A Norwegian kissed me and I don't know what to do

jladybugaboo: I am so not doing this.

goldstandard3000: He smooched me on my mouth parts and now I'm all confused

jladybugaboo: Confused doesn't rhyme with "to do."

goldstandard3000: I won't help Lydia write this song and now her rhymes are awful

jladybugaboo: If she keeps bugging me I'm going to do something unlawful

goldstandard3000: Rock and roll! New reputations! And Norwegian love!

jladybugaboo: Oh please someone come save me from all of the above!

Is it just me, or is everything getting more complicated?

It's definitely getting more interesting...

Acknowledgments

Mountains of thanks are due to the amazing people at Amulet books who have been so supportive of Lydia, Julie, and me: Susan Van Metre, James Armstrong, Melissa Arnst, Chris Blank, Chad Beckerman, Robyn Ng, Laura Mihalick, Morgan Dubin, and the inexhaustible Jason Wells. Vast oceans of gratitude and affection go to the Best Editor in the Whole Wide World Maggie Lehrman, who indulges my Need to Capitalize Very Important Words.

Thanks once more to the wonderful Dan Lazar, who always manages to respond to my weirdest wee hour emails with wit and grace, as well as Torie Doherty-Munro and all the fantastic people at Writers House.

Can I tell you what it's like to receive emails from readers all over the world? AMAZING. Thanks to all the readers and writers and librarians and booksellers and teachers who inspire me to work harder with their love and encouragement, and to my friends and family who inspired me to start writing and drawing in the first place.

And finally, thanks to my best friend and partner, Mark, who makes me dinner when I need to work in the evenings because I just need to color in this one last thing . . .

About the Author

Amy Ignatow is the author and illustrator of THE POPULARITY PAPERS series. She is a graduate of Moore College of Art and Design and was once a backup singer in a rock band called TODD YOUNG AND HIS ROCK BAND. Amy lives in Philadelphia with her husband, Mark, their daughter, Anya, and their cat, Mathilda, who is mellowing out despite herself. Kind of.

To Axi Nue, who knew a thing or two about reinvention,
and even more about rocking out.
—Ig

Artist's Note: The materials used to create the book are
ink, colored pencil, colored marker, yarn, and digital.

ISBN: 978-1-4197-0536-6

Text and illustrations copyright © 2013 Amy Ignatow
Book design by Amy Ignatow and Melissa Arnst

Printed and bound in China
10 9 8 7 6 5 4 3 2 1

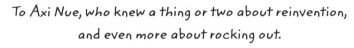

ABRAMS
THE ART OF BOOKS SINCE 1949

115 West 18th Street
New York, NY 10011
www.abramsbooks.com

Catch up with all of The Popularity Papers

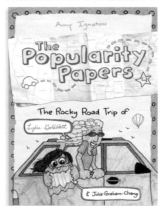

Also available in paperback!